65 Colours
of Rainbow

I0686877

65 Colours
of Rainbow

SMIT KAPILA

Srishti
PUBLISHERS & DISTRIBUTORS

SRISHTI PUBLISHERS & DISTRIBUTORS
Registered Office: N-16, C.R. Park
New Delhi – 110 019
Corporate Office: 212A, Peacock Lane
Shahpur Jat, New Delhi – 110 049
editorial@srishtipublishers.com

First published by
Srishti Publishers & Distributors in 2018

Text and illustrations copyright © Smit Kapila, 2018

10 9 8 7 6 5 4 3 2 1

This is a work of fiction. The characters, places, organisations and events described in this book are either a work of the author's imagination or have been used fictitiously. Any resemblance to people, living or dead, places, events, communities or organisations is purely coincidental.

The author asserts the moral right to be identified as the author of this work.

All rights reserved. No part of this publication may be reproduced, stored in a retrieval system, or transmitted, in any form or by any means, electronic, mechanical, photocopying, recording or otherwise, without the prior written permission of the Publishers.

Dedicated to
my family, friends and colleagues.

Contents

Introduction

In today's highly competitive world, I find that the life of an engineer is full of stress and work pressure. Since there is no way we can escape from our jobs, what we can do is make fun and laughter a part of our workplace. Well, all of us have our own funny workplace stories. The funny and weird incidents that take place at work always make us laugh and can lighten one's mood lessening the negative effects of work related stress on our minds.

This book will not give you ways to become successful but it will focus on making you understand on how to extract happiness, pleasure and joy from day to day incidents that take place around you at the workplace and how that can turn your workplace into a fun place.

I will share stories of my colleagues and friends and the weird, but funny incidents, that happened at their workplaces.

The Chip

The IT industry has expanded and grown enormously in the past few decades. Though, our older generation is not quite aware of this technology that we work on.

It was the month of July. This is the time of the year when engineers enter the real world leaving the dream world of their colleges behind.

One day, a new recruit, who had joined the organization just a week ago, arrived at the office in a furious state.

When asked the reason for his anger, he narrated this story. On his way to office, he had called up his native place which was somewhere in Punjab. His mother was enquiring about his general well being and so on. Very excited that he had joined one of the top IT giants in the country, he was sharing his experiences about his new job and people there. His mother, a homemaker, was not able to understand most of the 'jargon' that her 'grown up' son was using, and asked him to explain what kind of work he was involved in.

The guy told her with great pride, "Mom, I make (design is what he actually meant) chips. These are integrated circuits called ICs."

In the same breath, his mother replied, "Oh God! We put all our effort in making you an engineer and you are working in a chips factory making potato chips?"

Now, wasn't that a wonderful real life joke?

The Interview

My friend was not happy with the kind of work he was involved in the organization he was working in. Suffering from utter job dissatisfaction, he was looking for better opportunities elsewhere. He had already attended many interviews and although being quite intelligent and hard-working, luck was against him and things were not working out the way he wanted them to. This was taking a heavy toll on his morale and self-confidence.

One weekend, he went for yet another walk-in interview for a position which had been open for more than a month. As a pre-requisite, he had submitted four copies of his passport sized photograph at the beginning of the interview. The interview went rather well.

As a generic procedure, the interviewer asked, "Do you have any questions for us?"

My friend subtly replied, "I see that the position has been open for quite some time now. Approximately how many candidates would have appeared for the job?"

"Umm... around five hundred candidates," claimed the interviewer.

As soon as he heard this, my friend's attitude changed. He wanted all the four of his photographs, which he had submitted at beginning of the interview process, to be returned.

Stunned, the interviewer asked him the reason for the same. Well, the question was evident in his eyes as he was too stunned to speak!

My friend calmly said, "I have full confidence in myself and I don't want to let my photographs go to waste here. I can use them for some other interview.

The White Board

As an initiative for team bonding, improving inter-personal relationships and improving the presentation skills of the team, we used to have a team meeting once a week, generally on Fridays.

The team used to go out for lunch and play games. But apart from this, one team member, on a rotational basis, had to give a small presentation – be it general, technical or project related.

The conference rooms were used for this purpose. The speakers, to help explain their points, generally used the white board kept in the room.

One fine Friday, we had our colleague ready with his presentation. For better explanation of his topic on Team Work, he wanted to draw some diagrams on the board. He searched for the white board marker but couldn't find one there. Not wasting further time, he quickly went to his cabin and brought one.

The presentation went off rather well. At the end of it, the white board was full of diagrams, text and figures. Wrapping up with a quick question and answer session, the guy started clearing the board with the duster. But to his surprise the duster didn't seem to be doing its job at all. Not a dot was getting erased. He pressed it harder but in vain.

He picked up the marker that he had brought from his cabin and had a look at it. To his horror, on it was written 'Permanent Marker.' Well it took some effort and good 'team work' to get the board clean!

The Antivirus

One of my colleagues' friends, also from an IT company, told us about this interesting incident which happened at his work place.

One of his colleagues used to take a lot of time off from work. Every other day, he'd call his manager claiming he was sick and would skip work. His boss was extremely frustrated with him.

One day this fellow called his boss again saying, "I'll not be able to make it to office, I am not feeling well..."

Hearing this, his boss was absolutely mad and couldn't control his anger anymore.

He asked him sternly, "Just tell me what you are suffering from this time?

The guy replied, "I am down with viral fever."

The manager, hearing the same old excuse, said in a rage,

"And why is it that you catch the viral so often?"

The guy coolly replied, "Sir, I don't have a proper antivirus installed in my laptop...oops I mean in my body!"

Sleep

One of my 'scientist' friends was working in the R & D (Research and Development) unit of a product company. Like him, all his team mates were not only extremely intelligent but hard working as well. For them, it didn't matter whether it was day or night; if they had to finish something, they'd complete it before they left for home.

One of his team mates often used to work late hours. Since the place where he was staying was far off from the office, he used to sleep in the company's dormitory (well, the office was his second home anyway). Apart from the dormitory, he would sometime sleep on the table in one of the conference rooms. In this case, he would wake up very early at five the next morning, go to the dormitory, freshen up (he had kept his necessary accessories in the dormitory) and used to be back in office around nine in the morning.

One fine day (or night I should say!), he slept on the table in the conference room. He was really exhausted that day. The next morning he was literally half dead when he opened his eyes. To his surprise, or rather shock, the conference room was filled with people. His colleagues were sitting around him on their chairs while this fellow lay sprawled on the table in the centre of the conference room!

He is currently working with the Indian Space Research Organization.

The Busy Fellow

Ravi was quite a manipulator. He had good management skills – he could get his part of work done from others. And was able to show (or fool) the manager that he was the busiest person in the team. He used to keep his files scattered and disorganized occasionally to create a busy and 'involved completely in work' kind of impression.

Most of the time, he could be seen working on important looking pie charts, histograms, Pareto charts, graphs or some architecture diagrams/sequence diagrams with detailed flow.

One day, however it all came to an end. Good luck cannot favour one forever I suppose. He was playing online games as usual. When he saw the manager approaching, he immediately clicked on the 'Look Busy' tab. It was the web page which would direct him to some random auto generated graphs or architecture diagrams.

But this time, bad luck for him, the network became slow while he clicked on the 'Look Busy' tab. Suddenly a window popped up on his screen with a message that read:

Please wait, the 'Look Busy' page is getting loaded.

...And all this while his manager was standing behind his shoulder!

Since that incident, Ravi still looks very busy as he always used to. The only difference is that he is busy with 'real' work!

The Limping Leg

One of my friends' teammates was a wonderful actor. But what he had in acting skills, he lacked in brains. Here is the reason why:

Most of the IT companies under their HR policies allow employees to take a fixed number of sick leaves, which if not availed by the end of calendar year, get lapsed.

It was the month of December and this guy was still left with four unused sick leaves. A mysterious onslaught of illnesses is seen during the last few months of the year and many employees start taking leaves citing reasons such as fevers, headaches, the flu and the like.

This fellow however, wanted to be creative, different from the general lot. He didn't want to give any old excuse. He wanted to put his acting skills to use.

So, one day he came to office with his left leg limping badly. Good at acting, he made everyone, especially his boss believe his story of meeting with an accident. He said his bike had skidded and he had hurt his left leg.

Being clever, he made it a point to make it clear that it wasn't a fracture as he just wanted four days off. Gaining the sympathy of the boss, he happily got his sick leave without any fuss.

After four days, the guy was back in office. He was limping slightly now to keep his story authentic, pretending that he was a bit better. But to his surprise instead of receiving the 'How are you now?' greeting from the manager, he was met with 'Who are you...'

The reason? Well simple! He now had a limp in his right leg instead of the left. During the four days away, he had forgotten which leg had the limp originally.

What happened after that is another story!

The Break

It's a proven fact that all work and no play makes Jack a dull boy! This stands true for a workplace as well. For high productivity and efficiency, it is very important to take a small break every few hours.

All our breaks used to be team breaks. Be it a tea break, lunch break or even a news break, our team used to go together. It used to be a fun break with all of us sharing jokes and laughing uncontrollably.

During one such tea break, we were having a usual jokes and laughter session. Amongst us was a guy (one of my good friends) laughing loudly along with us. Since I didn't understand the joke told, I asked him to explain it to me and in a very casual manner, he replied, " Hey even I didn't understand the joke, I am laughing at yesterday's joke!"

Since then he was christened with the nickname 'Tubelight'. Although he was the 'brightest star' in our team, he could never ever escape from this tag.

The Toffee

Recently, one of my friends got a chance to go onsite to Finland. He was traveling for the first time in a plane. Sitting in the last seat, his heart sank when the plane took off but things became okay when the flight reached a cruising altitude. Then it was time for the in flight services to start.

A beautiful Finnish airhostess came over to his seat and offered him some toffees. They looked like white balls in their transparent wrappers with something written in Finnish. He was mesmerized by her beauty and the view from window – white clouds, like cotton, floating in the sky.

He tore off the plastic wrapper and put the toffee into his mouth. For ten minutes he kept chewing it, wondering why it was so tasteless. Since it was the first time he was tasting them, he thought, "Probably Finnish sweets taste bland like this."

Breakfast was served in a while which he relished thoroughly. After that there was silence in the plane as most of the passengers began to get ready for a nap while others put their headsets on.

He happened to look at the person sitting in the adjacent seat. This person, who had also taken two of the same 'tasteless' toffee, tore off their plastic wrappers and inserted the white balls into his ears. These were not toffees but cotton ear plugs!

My friend who now understood why the toffee he was chewing had been so tasteless and who was earlier praying for a safe journey, was now praying that nobody had seen him eating that 'toffee'!

The Training

All organizations spend a great deal of effort and resources on trainings.

Trainings span from a wide range of topics – from technical and management related, to behavioral and leadership. And the list goes on. Training sessions are not only a welcome respite from monotonous work, they are the main building blocks of the employee's personal development and stepping stones towards higher summits.

On a lighter note, the inevitable fact is that that it's hard to resist falling asleep in the course of these training sessions – especially the post lunch session. It's really hard to keep our eyes open. This being a known fact, the trainers try hard to make the session as interactive and interesting as possible so as to keep the audience alive!

My friend was nominated for a five day long leadership program. The session was aimed at building skills of upcoming leaders in the organization. The faculty used to keep the post lunch session extra interactive. They randomly asked questions and evaluated trainees on their grasping power.

At the end of one such post lunch session, the faculty was asking the audience questions. My friend, who was half asleep, was supposed to answer one of these quick questions. The answer he gave was a straightforward and simple 'no'. It was the correct answer. The trainer happily responded, "Good! Thanks for paying attention!"

My friend let out a sigh of relief and thought to himself, "My God! I didn't even hear the question. I thought he was asking if I understood the theory and I had said 'no'!

The Feedback

It's not only the boss, who appraises his reportees. It happens the other way round too. Almost all IT companies have a 360 degree feedback mechanism where the sub-ordinates evaluate their managers.

One of my friends from a startup IT company had to write a feedback about his manager. The manager used to sit in the same cubicle next to his seat.

Wary of what could happen if he wrote a negative feedback (which he wanted to) and his manager suddenly popped up and read it (which he knew was likely to happen), he was unable to think of a way to go about it.

Not having time to wait till the manager left by end of the day as he had to mandatorily submit the feedback by that afternoon, suddenly an idea flashed into his mind from one of the forwarded mails that he had received.

Very creative at writing, he gave the feedback which read something like this:

My manager does not
Behave like a boss and is always ready to
Co-operate with his sub-ordinates.
I would say,
If he continues managing our project, we'll not
Only feel happy but also
Be able to grow just like him.
Hope you understand our feelings and
So, we don't want to
Have any other manager apart from him, and always want to
Have him as our manager...

A second mail just mentioned: Read only the odd lines.

The Rest Room

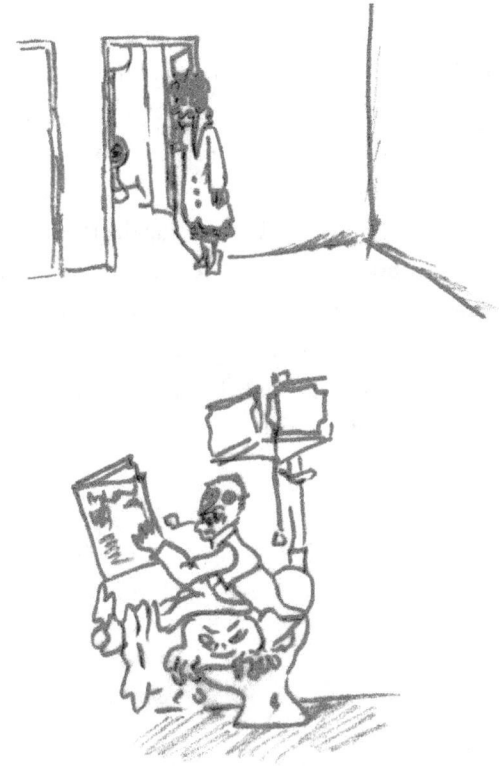

My friend, a design engineer, had an obsession – he loved reading books. At any given time, if he was not working, he would be reading. There would always be a book in his hand during tea time or any other break. He even used to take his books along while going to the rest room.

One day, he went to the loo, as usual, with a book in his hands. In a hurry, or most probably as he was pre-occupied with the thoughts of the next twists in the story, he just shut the door and forgot to lock it. He would be in there for no less than an hour.

During this time, one of his colleagues who had an upset stomach went running to the rest room. As good etiquette one would knock on a closed door to check if someone is inside, but if the door is open, it's but obvious that it would be vacant. So, seeing the toilet's door slightly open and assuming nobody was inside, he pushed the door wide open. Wide enough for everyone to see what was going on inside.

At that very moment, their group head entered the rest room and seeing the scene there, he just couldn't stop laughing! This must have been a better twist than his novel had.

The Telephone Call

Vishal was fresh out of campus and had joined the organization only a month back. He was working with the sales and marketing department.

This required a lot of interaction with various clients, customers and third party vendors. It was month end and as usual the work pressure was high. Every one was working late hours to meet the deadlines.

It was eight in the evening and Vishal had been working since the morning without a single break. He hadn't even had his lunch. To enquire about one of the open contracts, he had to call the president of a third party vendor. The president's name was Sashikant.

An exhausted Vishal dialed his number. He said,

"Hi, this is Sashikant here, can I talk to Vishal?"

Nobody knows what reply he got, but Vishal left the office that moment itself and was on leave for the next two days!

The Bluff

My friend narrated this hilarious incident. His project was ramping up and his team size was increasing with more and more freshers joining the company.

Since personal networking sites were blocked in their organization, the new guys, after receiving their corporate email ids, used it for personal interactions as well.

All the organizations have a support group which works specifically on filtering the emails and checking and controlling the spread of any virus in the company's network. Most of the spam emails (mostly containing .exe files) are blocked by this group, but still there are an 'intelligent few' which pass through that filter.

With a sudden expansion of the networking horizons, the freshers were on top of the world sharing their experiences and emailing activity was on a high. One day, a fresher was found sobbing at his desk. Trying to console him, my friend asked him the reason for his emotional burst. With tears in his eyes, the guy said,

"I got a popup message from the company's administrative department stating that my mails have been scanned and the contents of the mails were found to be offensive. It is also being noticed that I have been spending most of my time sending personal e-mails. So I will soon be shown the door."

Hearing this, my friend couldn't stop laughing. But seeing him surprised and rather annoyed with this response, my friend quickly took control of the situation and explained that this was just a bluff (mischief) done by the .exe file which probably got executed while opening one of his spam mails.

Profusely thanking my friend and visibly relieved, he sighed, "Oh! The execution of this file almost led to my execution!"

The Mail

A t work, group mails are the best alternative to a conference call or a Yahoo or Google chat, and the best way of keeping in touch with common friends. The group mail sessions indeed become quite interesting many a times. For example, when there is a conflict between two people and the rest take it upon themselves to add fuel to the fire!

My friend had this interesting story to tell. One such group mailing session, which he was part of, was going on in full flow. It seemed that everybody had no other work to do. The group mostly consisted of his class mates including many girls. Since everybody was using the 'reply to all' option, the mails were stacking up.

One of the members in this group was on leave that day. The next morning, when he was trying to open his mail box, it crashed. After quite an effort, he was able to retrieve his data. Once the mail box opened, he was stunned to find two hundred odd mails in his mail box (the reason why the mailbox crashed!).

After a little bit of scanning through the mails, he wrote a heated mail to the group member who had sent the maximum number of mails. The mail was full of the 'good' words that he had learnt in his entire life. But instead of clicking the 'Reply to' button, by mistake he clicked the 'Reply to all' button.

Well as expected, he never got a single mail from any girl since then.

The Party

Raghu, a senior from my college recollected this funny incident. He was a 1999 pass out. That was a boom period for the IT industry because of the Y2K uncertainties. Like all other IT companies, his organization was also reaping in high profits.

It was the month of January in 2000. The company's quarterly results were out, and since the quarter-on-quarter and year-on-year profits were way above the target, as a gesture towards its employees, the company threw a grand party. For alcohol lovers, there were free drinks from the best brands to savour.

It was late in the night. Raghu and his team mates had had a lot of drinks and were out of their senses too. They (my senior and his colleague) had their eyes closed and were having a philosophical discussion on some topic. They continued talking for one hour, and when Raghu opened his eyes, he noticed that his colleague's face had changed.

It was someone else sitting next to him. He didn't know where and when his colleague had disappeared and was replaced by this stranger who took over and continued the 'philosophical discussion' they were having. They had never met each other, never seen each other but were talking to each other for more than an hour.

They are the best of friends now!

Team Work

The first learning that one gets from induction training is the importance of team work. It's the team work that makes a project a success or a failure.

This incident is a wonderful example of team work. My ex-roommate was working in a small startup company. His was a team of five which included one girl. Since the girl was a lateral joinee, and all the four guys had worked together for more than a year, the bonding was great amongst the guys.

One of these guys received a dubious email. After reading it, he couldn't resist sharing it with his colleagues. He immediately called all three guys to his cabin and asked them to read it on his PC screen. Suddenly this girl entered his cabin.

In a state of shock and not knowing what to do, all four of them stood up and hugged the PC monitor from all sides so that nothing was visible. The girl was mature and intelligent enough to understand what was going on, so she left the cabin at once.

Well, wasn't that good team work?

The Pantry

It was the first day at work for Anil. He was one of the five new joinees in a team. Their manager introduced him to the other team members and walked them around the campus premises, showing them the pantry, canteen, library, gymnasium, playroom and other important locations in the premises.

It would take at least two days for their PC allotment and a desk allocation so the team spent this time reading books in the library.

Taking a break, Anil and his friend went to the pantry. The pantry had an automated tea and coffee maker. There was also provision for making tea to your own taste. An electric heater, along with sugar and milk were provided.

There was a person already standing inside the pantry brewing some tea. These guys assumed that he was the pantry guy, and asked him to make two more cups of tea for them. The gentleman did so, and handed two cups of tea to them.

When these guys were having the last sip and were about to leave, the person said,"Welcome to our organization! I am the vice-president of this company. Hope the tea was nice and hope you have a nice time here!"

The Transfer

Volatility is an inevitable part of IT industries. Projects, departments, even companies get scrapped based on market and financial swings.

Kunal was part of a small R&D group in his company. They were involved in creating innovative designs and products to keep the organization at its competitive edge. But because of the looming clouds of recession, their team was directed to be moved to other more profitable departments of the organization.

Being the best in class, all the five members of this team were absorbed in various departments and all of them promoted with large teams reporting to them.

Kunal called his mother to share the news of his promotion. Just to give an overview of how it happened, he started explaining to her about the closure of the R&D group, the movement and so on.

Not listening to or rather not understanding the complete story, and just picking the 'closed' and 'moved', his mother started crying. Sobbing she said, "My son, what will you do now? Didn't you perform well enough? Did you fight with your manager?"

Not wanting to explain everything again to his sobbing mother, he shouted, "Mom, listen! I was just joking. Forget what I said. Please buy some sweets for yourself, I have been promoted!

The Couple

A mongst one of the ways to curb attrition, many organizations provide greater incentives for couples. Both a husband and a wife working in the same company have more stability and are less likely to wander outside.

Gaurav, quite an extrovert by nature, had moved to a new project and a new team. It was a big account with the head count exceeding hundred. It took him just few days to win the hearts of his new team members and he was soon one of the most popular guys in the team.

One week had passed since Gaurav had joined this new account. The 'all boys' group went out for a tea break. This time a new member, Amit, had joined them for tea. He had been on leave the previous week and so Gaurav had not been introduced to him. As usual, whatever topic they started with, the conversation would end up with discussions on the 'good looking girls' in their account.

Completely involved in the discussion, Gaurav started talking about one particular girl whom he had just seen that morning. He exclaimed, "Oh god! She is so gorgeous, where was she all this while?" While he was speaking, Amit's face turned red and the smiles of all the others vanished.

Before he could utter one more word, someone pulled him and whispered into his ears, "The girl you are talking about is Amit's wife!"

The Badge

As a company's security policy, all its employees are required to wear ID (Identity Card) badges with their recent photos on them.

Rahul had just arrived in the office. It was a dry and dusty morning and since he had ridden his bike without a helmet, Rahul went to wash his face. He took off his ID badge, kept it on his desk and went to the wash room. After returning, he wore his badge again.

The day went by as usual apart from the fact that few people were giving him strange looks when he went for his lunch and tea breaks. Nevertheless, he didn't pay much attention to them and carried on with his routine activities.

The next morning, while he was going through the scrutiny check to enter the main gate of the premises of the company, he was stopped by the security guard on duty.

Annoyed, he shouted at the guard saying, "Can't you see I am wearing my badge? What else you need?" The guard calmly replied, "Sir, the photograph on your ID doesn't match with your face."

In surprise, Rahul looked at his ID. He was shocked to see that there was a monkey's face in place of his own. With a little effort, he carefully scratched the 'monkey's face' and slowly his face reappeared on the ID. The guard had got the reassurance he wanted, but Rahul could never find out who had turned him into a monkey!

The Marriage

Rajeev was always in a rush. Restless by nature, he couldn't stay at a place for more than five minutes. At the same time, he had the extra gray matter in his head to compensate for his shortcoming.

While typing, he would make so much noise, it felt as if the keys were popping out of the keyboard. Still worse was his habit of opening the door by pushing it hard with both his hands. Many a times, he was advised (or rather warned!) not to do that. But he heeded to none of the requests or warnings.

One day, as usual, he was rushing towards his colleague's cabin. But on the way, someone called out to him. He was busy replying to the fellow, without looking towards the door. Then as was his habit, he put out both his hands to push open the door. A lady colleague who was just coming out of that cabin opened the door and at that very moment this guy's hands reached out towards the door, assuming that it was closed.

Now what happened next can't be explained here but, the two got married the very next month.

The Tape Recorder

In this world of modern and hi tech gadgets, a tape recorder is a thing of the past. However the nostalgia of the good old days returns when Shubham is in the vicinity. The reason is simple. He has some pre-recorded phrases mapped in his memory.

Ask him a particular question, and the answer will always be the same as though you have pressed the 'play' button of a tape recorder.

Another stark similarity with tape recorder is that the 'content' of his voice will always be the same; but only the voice quality will vary according to the state of the 'head'.

A few questions and his 'recorded' replies:

- Any question related to work

  Shubham: "Hey man, too much work! Yesterday I was working till late at night. I think today I'll not be able to leave early either." (But yesterday he was seen leaving by the 6'o clock shuttle!)

- Any question related to life

  Shubham: "Life is junk man!" (Even though he got a salary hike that day!)

- Any question related to a movie

  Shubham: "This is the worst movie that I have ever seen!" (But you heard him cheering inside the theatre!)

The Boss

IT companies are wonderful examples of places of 'national integrity'. People from different regions and following different religions work together as a team.

Prem was from Punjab and had joined a company in Bangalore. This was his first visit to the southern part of the country. Prem, also fondly called 'Singh', was popular amongst his team members. The team also comprised of engineers from different states.

Two of his team mates were from Kerala and he was learning Malayalam from them. Prem had noticed that when these two guys were talking to each other in Malayalee, they used one particular word very frequently. He asked them the meaning of that word and they said that it meant, 'You are great.'

That moment his boss (also from Kerala) entered the cabin, and thinking that the boss would appreciate his gesture in Malayalee, Prem complimented him with that word. The boss' face turned pink and he abruptly left the cabin.

When he narrated the scene, his teammates told him the actual meaning of the word. It wasn't a compliment at all, but the most abusive word in Malayalee. Although his manager didn't show any sign of bitterness, Prem was constantly worried that despite his hard work, his appraisal would get affected because of this.

All his apprehensions vanished when he got the best rating during the appraisals!

The Loo

R aja, after working for five years as a developer, had recently taken up a pre-sales role in another organization. This new job required lots of traveling and client visits both in India and abroad.

He had one such visit to a client's location in Texas. It was supposed to be a a day long visit where he had few proposals to discuss with various managers.

It was a tough client to deal with and Raja was a little nervous on how the client's response would be. It was very important for him to clinch this deal as the end of the financial year was close and targets had to be met.

Raja was all prepared for the 'big' meeting but somewhere down inside, he feared the worse! Under stress, Raja was frequenting the rest room every five minutes.

When he reached the client's place and was about to start his presentation, he felt the need to relax and went to the loo once again. While he was standing at the urinal, he noticed that something was written on the wall above the urinal in front of him.

He couldn't stop laughing when he read it:

Please come closer, it's shorter than you think!

All his anxiety vanished and the deal was clinched!

The Philosopher

In every company you'll find people who are always lost in their own world. They basically live in two worlds: Physically in the real world but mentally in the world of their own thoughts.

Suri used to be one such person. Suri and his team used to have lunch in the company's cafeteria. Suri, while having his food, would be present physically in the group, but his mind would be wandering somewhere else.

Lost in his thoughts, this guy, almost every other day, after having lunch, used to take his used plate to the hand wash room instead of the dish washer room. That was not new or surprising.

One fine day, as usual after finishing lunch, every body was taking their used plates and glasses to the dish washer room. Suri was also with them.

While going to the dish washer room, the group realized that the other people in the canteen were laughing at them. They turned to look at Suri who seemed to be drawing all the attention.

He was holding the jug of water in his hand in place of his used glass!

The Drive

This incident is one of the most dangerous and weird ones that I've come across. Rajesh and Suraj were working in the same company and were roommates as well.

It was a big day for their organization (and of course for them too!) as the company had got listed in the New York Stock Exchange (NYSE). A big party was organized by the company for its employees. After the big bash it was time for the guys to return home. Both Rajesh and Suraj were completely drunk, and although they were advised not to drive in such an inebriated condition, they paid no heed and drove off on their bike.

Rajesh was driving and Suraj was the pillion rider. After reaching home, Rajesh parked the bike in the garage, unlocked the door and fell flat on his bed. Suddenly, he realized that something was missing – Suraj!

He remembered that Suraj had been sitting on the bike when they had started off! He quickly regained his senses. He looked for Suraj in the garage, and in the neighborhood but in vain. He then went back in search of him, using the same route that they had taken while coming. At one sharp turn, he found Suraj lying on the road side.

Suraj had fallen asleep while sitting on the bike, and around that sharp turn, he had fallen off the bike! He was one lucky guy to have escaped without any injuries.

Now the two of them have stopped driving instead of drinking!

The VNC

There is a well known saying: 'Whatever happens, happens for our own good'. During the testing phase of a project, engineers need to switch between various work locations. For example, the work station might be at one location, while the testing lab may be at a different location.

Tanu was carrying out the system testing of a product that her team had designed. Her work cabin was on the ground floor and the test lab was on the third floor. For various reasons one needed to keep going back and forth between these locations.

Since this frequent movement was difficult, software geeks have developed a wonderful software called VNC (virtual network). As the name suggests, one can take control of the PC located at a remote location from your work PC.

Tanu was making full use of this software. She would just run it on both the PCs, sit in her cabin, take virtual control of the PC in the lab and complete the required testing without any discomfort. After running this software, the work PC would virtually behave as the lab PC (which was to be remotely controlled). That is, whatever one was typing/browsing on the work PC was being actually typed/browsed on the remote PC. VNC could be switched on or off as per requirement (to release control).

One day, Tanu was sitting at her workplace and typing an email. She had forgotten to switch off the VNC and was virtually typing on the lab PC. It was her bad luck that her boss was sitting in the lab and she was unaware of that. She was writing a mail to her friend expressing her wish for a job change. The reason she stated was the meager salary.

She also mentioned that she somehow couldn't talk to her manager regarding this. So the only way out for her was to directly look out for opportunities outside.

Her boss read the whole mail while she was absolutely clueless. He immediately called her to his cabin.

After five minutes she came out with a stunned face, holding a letter. She had got a big salary hike!

The Atheist

Recently, the IT sector has been gripped by recession. One of my friends, working with an IT company in Bangalore, recently became a Project Manager. He had a team of four engineers reporting to him.

He had directions from the human resource team to reduce the team size and relieve (lay off) one engineer. New to a PM's role, and not used to firing employees earlier, he had a hard time deciding how to go about it. The reason was that all the four engineers were absolute gems. All of them very hardworking, very smart, talented and skilled in their professional fields.

Looking into the past records of all four of them, and on the basis on various performance criteria, he finally got down to two engineers (a guy and a girl), on one of whom the axe had to fall.

Not able to further nail down on one of these two, he stopped using his brain and resorted to the policy of 'first come first serve'. Whoever showed a loose end first would be the one to go.

Under pressure from the management to give his decision in two days' time, he decided that whosoever came late to office would be the 'one'.

Surprisingly both of them entered the office together! Okay, the boss thought – Plan B. Whoever takes more time off for breaks would go. But to his surprise, both of them went together for tea breaks, lunch breaks and spent equal time off from active work. They even left the office together.

Having no clue what to do next, he (remember he was an atheist!) prayed to God to help him out. The very next day both the engineers came to his desk for a discussion. The two were getting married to each other. And the girl wanted to submit her resignation letter!

My friend has been a God fearing person since then.

The Compilation

Abhinav got selected by a leading organization during the campus recruitments in his college. A year later, when he completed his engineering course, he was all set to start his career in the field of Information Technology.

The first week he went through all sorts of training including induction training and basic technical training. The next week onwards, he dived straight into the job. He became part of a team which was handling a small software development project.

For hands-on training, he was given an assignment – to compile and build a C program (most of the coding had already been done by someone else). While compiling the code, he was getting lots of errors. Unable to understand the complex code and solve the errors, he just started commenting on the parts of the code displaying errors.

Finally he was able to compile the code successfully. Excited, he showed the compiled code to his teammate.

Laughing out loud, his teammate said, "Great job done. You have compiled all the 'comments' successfully!"

The Microphone

Hari and his teammates were attending a training program on his company's policies and standards. The trainer had a wireless microphone clipped on to his shirt. A permanent wireless receiver and the amplifiers connected to the speakers were kept at the back of the room.

After three hours of a continuous 'sleep inducing' session, they had a tea break. Since there were still some trainees who were inside the room who didn't go out for tea, the speaker went outside to make a call during this tea break.

On phone he was grumbling, "I am fed up of giving this same training again and again…"

After the fifteen minute break was over, he returned to the training room. Before he could start the session, all the people stood up and in sync shouted, "Even we are fed up of being given the training again and again!" This was followed by a wave of laughter as the faculty stared at them spell bound.

He had forgotten to switch off the mic and whatever he was saying on the phone, had reverberated in the whole room!

The Bus

Although Rajneesh was staying just five kilometers away from his work location, he preferred to use the company bus to commute rather than drive his own car because of the frequent traffic jams on the way.

Since the shuttle service was frequent, about every hour, till midnight, he didn't have to worry about the time he left office. Of late there was a sudden surge of work load and he had been leaving late from office. One day, he caught the 11 p.m. shuttle. This was a long route shuttle with the destination forty kilometres away from the office. His house fell on that route, only five kilometres away from the office.

Exhausted after the long day at work, he fell asleep the moment he sat in the bus. His exhaustion was evident from his loud snores. Suddenly someone shook him awake and he heard the words, "Sir, this is the last stop. Please get down."

He had missed his stop! It was midnight and the place was in the outskirts of the city, totally unknown to him. He looked for an auto-rickshaw but in vain.

Feeling sorry for him, the driver of the bus invited him to his temporary house – the bus! He slept there and in morning had breakfast with the driver. He went back to the office in the same bus. Well it was certainly a wonderful experience, wasn't it?

The Shy Guy

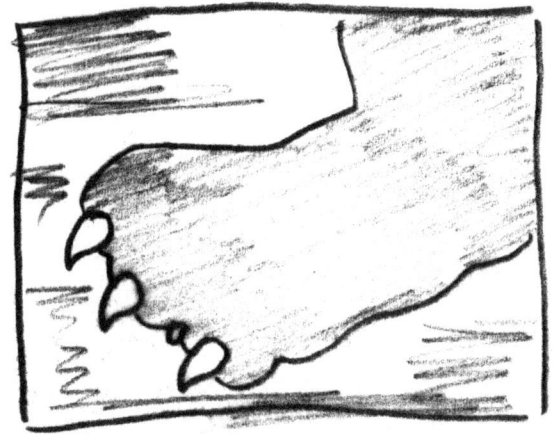

Ishaan had recently shifted to a company in Bangalore for better compensation. He was from Delhi and had had lots of girlfriends there. But soon the 'out of sight - out of mind' theory worked against him and he lost touch with all his old girlfriends.

Desperately looking for a good girl to make friends with, he talked to many girls but after a little interaction, he would come to know that the girl was either already engaged or worse, already married. Though his impression was not that bad (he never misbehaved with anyone), he was known to be a big flirt.

But of late, things had changed. Ishaan had changed. Whenever a girl used to pass by, or was in front him, he never used to look up at her face, but rather kept his head down looking towards the floor. Everybody wondered why he had suddenly become so shy, and couldn't even look up straight at a girl's face.

What they didn't know was that he wasn't looking down because he was shy. The fact was that he used to look down at a girls' feet to see if they were wearing any toe rings because he had been told by someone that according to South Indian tradition, married girls wore rings on their toes!

The Hands Free

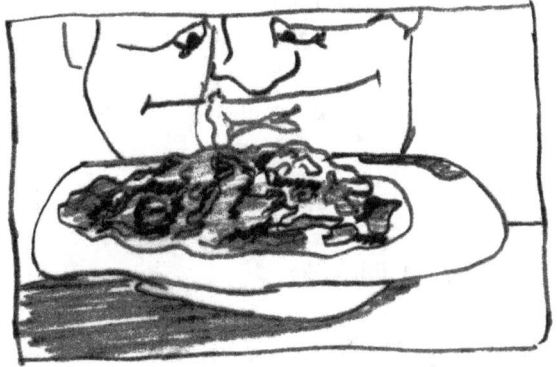

If Sushant had not been a software engineer, he would have been a call operator for a simple reason – every two minutes he used to get a call. Since it was difficult to hold the mobile in his hands all the time, he used his hands free most of the times. Since he had long hair, the bluetooth device in his ear was not easily visible.

Quite often, he would be sitting on his seat, in front of his PC and talking to someone.

Suddenly he'd ask a question aloud. For example, "When will you be leaving today?" Thinking that he was talking to his colleagues sitting next to him, they would reply. As they'd get no response from him they'd realize that he was on his hands free talking to someone on the phone.

Once when he got a call during lunch time, he switched on his bluetooth. He continued eating though as his hands were free. His teammates knew he was talking on the phone, but controlled their laughter so that Sushant wouldn't come to know what was happening as they noticed the surprised passersby, giving strange looks at this fellow, who was continuously talking, looking at his plate, smiling, making faces, as if he was talking to the food on his plate.

Snippets of his conversations with his food (from an onlooker's perspective):

Sushant (surprised): "What is this?"

Eating his food

Sushant (angry): "I didn't like it."

Eating his food

Sushant (smiling): "Wow... You are too sweet!"

Eating his food

The Chatting

Prakash was known for multi-tasking. His teammates claimed he had a 'dual processor' in his brain. Prakash made full use of this god gifted talent. He could keep talking to someone on the phone and still continue his 'coding' work. He also used to chat a lot with his friends online on messenger. But this never affected his productivity and that was the reason he could manage to retain his job in his company. Nevertheless, he made sure his manager didn't get to know about this as chatting was not allowed in the company.

One day, during office hours, he was so engrossed chatting with his friend that he didn't realize that his manager was approaching his cubicle. His manager saw him chatting, but before he could read anything, Prakash saw him and closed the chat window in the nick of time.

Before the boss had arrived, the message from the other end was: *"Why did you make such a big issue out of it?"*

Suddenly a message from the other end popped up (since Prakash had stopped typing for sometime): *"Are you there?"*

Prakash realized the gravity of the situation and quickly rephrased the sentence that he was about to type. It went something like this:

Prakash: *"Wait, I am just looking into the design."*

From the other end: *"???"*

Prakash: *"We should be able to resolve this issue."*

From the other end: *"Yes, I completely agree with you."*

Prakash: *"Okay, let's meet for this tomorrow."*

From the other end: *"Ya, sure"*

Prakash: *"See you tomorrow then, bye"*

From other end: *"Bye."*

Since his manager was not aware of the subject, Prakash told him that he was chatting with a vendor. There was 'an issue' with the design, and he was discussing that with the vendor's support team.

The boss appreciated Prakash's dedication towards the project and his novel idea of 'chatting' to get things done faster!

The Coupon

If Nitin had not been an engineer, he would have been a philosopher. He was never present in the real world, and had to be brought back by external forces, i.e. his colleagues!

Being a bachelor, Nitin would have his breakfast as well as lunch in office. It was better to arrive a little early as the queue used to be shorter. There was a coupon system in the canteen. The coupon bought from the billing counter had to be handed over to the waiters serving the food.

That day, as usual, the buffet was laid out. The spoons though, were kept at the very beginning, so everyone was picking a spoon first and moving forward in the queue. Nitin, when his turn came, absentmindedly offered a spoon instead of the coupon to the guy serving food.

Waiting for sometime, and still not receiving his meals, he asked the waiter the reason for the same.

The waiter candidly replied, "Sir, I want the coupon, not the spoon! You give me the coupon and I'll give you your meal!"

The Lift

S ailesh and Gurmeet were roommates and working for the same organization, although their departments were different. Sailesh was into finance management, while Gurmeet was a hard core software engineer.

After watching a late night movie show on Sunday, they were both not able to wake up on time the next morning and missed the company bus. They had no option now but to use public transportation to reach office.

While they were waiting for an auto rickshaw, a car came to a screeching halt and stopped just in front of them. The driver of the car greeted Gurmeet and both of them shook hands. He offered them a lift and both the guys sat in the car.

Sailesh had not met this guy before, but could make out that he was Gurmeet's colleague. Although he was not formally introduced to this guy, their interaction started after some time.

After opening up a little bit, Sailesh said, "Thank god we got a lift. I had an important meeting today. These bosses, you know, should be kicked hard. Without any reason, my boss fixes a meeting so early. If I get a chance, I would shoot all the bosses in this world!"

Well, he would have held his tongue if he knew that the driver of the car was Gurmeet's boss!

The Love Story

This one is a simple but strange love story. Pramod had good communication skills, both oral as well as written. But what he lacked was patience. Once he had written something he would not review or re-read it, and he'd simply click the 'send' button. Many a times, the mail would bounce back as the email ids would be typed incorrectly.

For official mails, he'd start with the usual greetings and finish the draft with commoners like 'regards ' and his auto signature. However for personal mails, he would replace 'regards' with 'love' for close friends and relations.

One day he was writing an official mail to one of his lady colleagues but instead of writing 'regards, Pramod', by mistake he wrote 'love, Pramod'.

As usual, he gave it no second thought and clicked on the 'send' button. Then suddenly he realized what he had written. He feared what her response would be but to his surprise, the mail she wrote back was signed 'love, Reshma'. And that was the beginning of an eternal love story!

The Printout

Each one of us has heard the phrase 'blessing in disguise'. This incident is a wonderful example. One of my friends was frustrated over his salary package. He was a critical resource of his team and could easily pressurize his manager for an increment. But he never did so. Instead he started looking for other options.

He touched base with various consultants and started attending interviews. For one such interview, he had to take a printout of the 'confirmatory mail' that he had received from the consultant.

During lunch time, assuming that nobody was around, he fired a print out of that mail. But to his horror, his manager suddenly appeared from nowhere and stood near the printer waiting for a print job that he had given.

While the manager was waiting for his own print job, he saw the printout on the printer stating:

'Dear Mr Punit, as discussed on the phone, we confirm your interview date and time as .... Please make yourself available for the same.'

The manager called him immediately, had a discussion with him, and the very next day he got an increment letter.

The Sick Leave

It was the month of November. The calendar year was coming to an end. Everybody wanted to utilize their quota of sick leaves.

My friend worked in a team of five. One fine day, co-incidentally, all his colleagues took leave from work the same day. They were all sick. After a day of rest, all of them were back in office the next day. The boss, having his complete team back at work, called a team meeting. At this time, none of the team members knew that all the others had also gone on leave.

The boss greeted all his team members and enquired about their health. Everyone looked a little surprised at boss' behavior as he was not known to be so caring and warm hearted. Nevertheless, after he individually conversed with each one of them, he made this statement,

"See what a co-incidence, all of you were on sick leave because of falling – "Amit was on leave because he fell down the stairs, Sunil was on leave because he fell in the bathroom, Kishore fell in the kitchen, and Nathan fell off his bike. Thank god nobody was on leave because of falling in love!"

Nobody in the team fell sick for the next one year!

The Mobile

Kulbir was fond of cell phones. Every two months or so he would replace his mobile. He would be the first one to register for new launches as well. With his humongous contact list and with many contacts with same names, he used to tag the chosen ones with special names instead of their original names.

Always worried about the security and safety of his new assets, his phones had the best of the authentication and locking features.

But none of these could save him from what was going to happen next.

Kulbir had recently uploaded a new caller tune on his cell and his colleagues were listening to it. His manager also arrived and joined the group. He also wanted to hear the tone again. He used an easy way to do that. He called Kulbir's number from his own cell so that he could hear the tone when his phone rang.

While Kulbir's phone was ringing, his manager took the phone from him to have a look at it as it was one of the latest models. But the moment he held the phone in his hands, his face turned pale.

On the screen of the phone was flashing 'Devil calling'!

The Job Portal

Sanjeev was fed up of coding all the time. It had been two years since he had joined and he had been doing the same monotonous work. Since there was no visibility for a possible role change in his company, he started considering opportunities elsewhere.

He didn't have an internet connection at home, and had no time to go to an internet café so he was using his work PC in the office for job hunting. As a background activity, he always had some job portal opened up.

Since it was dangerous to browse these portals in office as his manager could come to know that he was looking for a job change, he was always extra cautious not to leave his PC unlocked in his absence.

Once, however, it happened that he got a call on his mobile and since the signal was weak inside his cubicle, he went out to attend the call. He forgot to lock his PC and the job portal was open on his PC. As luck would have it, his manager came to his seat for a query, and happened to notice his monitor. After he returned, he was called by his manager. No questions asked, his manager said,

"Hey Sanjeev, why are you looking for a job in embedded? The telecom domain has much better scope."

Stunned at his manager's question, he quickly made up a story and said, "Thanks for your advice; I was actually doing this for my friend."

Throwing a silent bomb, his manager said, "Well I guess, your friend might miss you so why don't you join him as well!"

The SMS

Pavan's team had gone to one of the city's best clubs for a team outing. Volunteers from the team had organized a lot of team activities: Tug of war, Antakshri and many more. After sunset the bachelors, particularly the guys who used to 'drink occasionally', couldn't resist and decided to go to the bar.

Since drinks were not part of the team budget, they decided to have them and pay from their own pockets. Pavan, after quite a few pegs, while trying hard to remain seated and keep his balance, received an SMS on his cell phone. The first time everyone ignored it, but when there were two or three more SMSs subsequently, his friends couldn't let it go.

They started teasing him that the messages were from his girlfriend though they had no idea whether he had a girlfriend or not. Although Pavan tried his best to evade this question, they kept bugging him.

Pavan, who had always given an impression that he was never interested in making girlfriends, thought that if he was able to convince them that the message was from one of his 'male' friends, the issue would die down. In an inebriated state, this is how he offered an explanation," My dear friends, it's not like what you are thinking, actually 'she' is a male!"

The April Fool

It was the 1st of April, famously known as April Fool's Day. Sandy, ever ready to do something naughty, could never let this day go without making a fool of someone.

His colleagues had already been his victims on previous occasions and this time he wanted to do something big. He wanted to go for someone big.

"Okay! Let it be the boss this time," he declared. There was no personal grudge with his boss nor did he have any selfish motive behind it, it was just for fun's sake.

He wrote a resignation letter stating that he was not happy with his current salary and wanted to quit. As per his plan, he handed over his resignation letter to his boss and walked out of his cabin.

As expected, after some time, his boss called him in for a discussion. But before Sandy could tell him the real story, his boss placed a letter in his hand. He read the letter, shook hands with his boss and 'quietly' came out of his cabin.

The letter had his new salary structure with a twenty percent raise!

His boss not only became an 'April Fool' but a 'real fool' as well!

The Festival

It was Holi, the festival of colours. Manjunath used to visit his home town every year during the festive season and used to have a colourful celebration there.

This year, however, he couldn't make it to his native town. A little depressed, Manjunath first decided to take a day off from office and stay at home on this day. But suddenly an idea struck his mind. He decided to celebrate this festival with his friends and colleagues in office.

To induce the festive spirit, he brought some sweets mixed with a little *bhang* to the office. He offered the sweets to his team mates and his boss, but he himself did not have any, so that he could enjoy the 'real life drama' that was going to unfold!

After a few minutes, the scene in the office was totally topsy-turvy. His boss started typing a mail which was never ending. One of his team mates started printing the same document again and again. As the time passed, the effect of the bhang reduced and every one slowly returned to their normal state.

By this time, the boss had already written a twenty page long mail and a team mate had taken a hundred printouts of the same document!

The Toothpaste

Kartik didn't have his own conveyance and relied on the company shuttle for transportation to office. It was important to catch the company bus in the morning as there was no other shuttle till late afternoon. If he missed it, the only other way was to take an auto-rickshaw or a cab which would not be a viable option as it was too expensive.

There was always a time crunch in the morning. Either you wake up early and have enough time to get ready or enjoy your sleep for as long as you can and 'speed up' the process of freshening up. The second option obviously was more luring. He used to wake up as late as possible, get ready in split seconds and rush off to catch the bus.

One day, during this rush hour, while he was brushing his teeth with a new tooth paste, (since he didn't buy it, he assumed that his roommate must have got it,) he felt the foam produced was much more than usual. He rinsed his mouth with water many a times but the foam just kept coming out from 'nowhere'.

Wondering which new brand of tooth paste his roommate had bought, he picked it up again and was shocked when along with its brand's name, he read the tag line 'For a wonderful shaving experience'!

The Reply

Mohit had recently joined a customer support team for one of the products that his company was manufacturing.

Here, amongst various factors, the growth depended on how many customer calls were attended to in a given amount of time, how fast the customer complaint was resolved and to what extent the customer was satisfied with the interaction or the response they had got.

Mohit was doing quite well. He had picked up the correct ways to deal with various types of customers. Every time Mohit used to receive a customer call, he started the interaction with a general greeting, "Hello! This is Mohit here, what can I do for you?"

One day, Mohit had a big fight with his manager. The moment he was back at his desk, he received a customer call. He picked up the phone and answered, "Hello! This is Mohit here, what *the hell* can I do for you?"

And the customer aptly responded, "Go to hell!"

The Draft

Sunita was looking for a job change, so she was writing to various consultants, forwarding her resume to them. She had also managed to get the e-mail ids of the HR contacts of various companies. So now she could even directly write to these HR personnel.

She drafted a generic mail and by just editing the name of the person she was writing to, she could use the same draft for different companies. This saved her the extra effort of writing a long mail again and again.

Wondering why she was not getting response to any of her mails, she wrote back to one of the HR but was stunned to get the response- "While trying to move forward in life, you have used the 'Forward' button in your mail box a bit more than you should! Her mail, as received by HR personnel was 'forwarded' back to her as well.

Hi Deepak, please find my resume attached along with. It'll be my pleasure to work with your esteemed company...
In anticipation of a positive response,
Thanks,
Sunita
.... forwarded message ....
Hi Tanya, please find my resume attached along with. It'll be my pleasure to work with your esteemed company...
In anticipation of a positive response,
Thanks,
Sunita

.... forwarded message ....
Hi Vaani, please find my resume attached along with. It'll be my pleasure to work with your esteemed company...
In anticipation of a positive response,
Thanks,
Sunita

The Roman

Jatin was quite an intellectual person. He used to be the energy source for whichever team he was working with. However, he was impressionable and used to get carried away very quickly.

Let me give you a few examples. If his teammates were buying Nokia cell phones, he would throw his current phone away and buy himself a Nokia model. If his friends were leaving late, he too would stay back in office. If his colleagues chose for a new plan from Airtel, he too would cancel his current plan, and would activate the same one!

But once he took it too far. In a short span of time, four of his colleagues, some of who were his good friends, left the company and joined other places. Though he personally was satisfied with the job, he couldn't negate the fact that his four colleagues had left.

So he went ahead and submitted his resignation. During the exit interview, he was asked the reason for his parting ways with the organization. He replied, "I believe in the proverb, 'In Rome do as Romans do'. My colleagues are leaving the company and so must I!"

The HR manager who was taking the exit interview and had expected a 'salary hike' or 'location change' or 'bad boss' or 'job satisfaction' or any of the usual reasons, was stunned to hear this response. It was definitely a first!

The Accident

M ost of the people will agree with this statement: People who drink or smoke together are best of the friends. Smoking and drinking together strengthens the bond of their friendship.

Anurag, a chain smoker, was a rash driver. Everybody was afraid to get on his bike. The number of accidents he was involved in was high, although by God's grace, he was never critically injured.

One day, he was driving out of his office premises towards the main road. The moment he got on the main road, he collided head on with another biker. Both of them fell down and sustained minor injuries. This led to a verbal spat between them.

During the brawl, Anurag, suddenly asked the other person, "Do you smoke?" The other fellow paused and then nodded his head. Soon after they went to the near by shop and had a good smoking session together.

They parted ways with a hearty handshake. Had there been an accident?!

The TCON

Neha, a project leader, was handling a project from a Japanese client. The Japanese, known to be hard working, were driving the team to the limits. Since the project was in a critical phase, they were having daily telephonic conference calls (TCON) with the client.

One of the most difficult parts of these conference calls was the language issue. The Japanese were not good at English and used to speak English with a Japanese accent that was difficult to grasp.

During one such TCON, Neha and her complete team were discussing a new requirement that had to be added in the design.

Neha pressed the 'mute' button on the phone and started discussing with her team members on the technical aspects of this new requirement that had come from the client. However, to lighten up the mood, she suddenly started mimicking the client's Japanese accent. She was making up her own words which sounded like Japanese. And suddenly a voice from the phone reverberated in the room saying, "Hey Neha it's not 'kyuni chirwa', it's 'konni chiwa'." (Konni-chiwa means 'hello' in Japanese).

Neha had not pressed the mute button properly and the client had been listening to everything!

The Explanation

As far as his family knew him, Subranil was a teetotaler, and to his close friends he was an occasional drinker. But in reality he was a hard core alcohol loving man. However his colleagues didn't know of this 'reality'. But this was just one part of him. On the whole he was a wonderful person and in many terms, there could not be a better person than him. He was quite popular amongst his teammates too. His wonderful sense of humor and childish behavior was well loved.

Subranil's colleague was getting married and during his bachelor's party, all the male members in his team were present. Subranil enjoyed his drinks along with everyone else. After sometime, he fell flat on the floor. His friends helped him get back to some state of 'normality' and dropped him home.

The next day when he entered the office, many questioning eyes were pointing at him. And he knew what the question was – What happened last night?" Subranil came up with an explanation. He said,

"Hey guys, I am sorry for yesterday's incident. Actually, I drank for the first time so that happened."

Looking at his innocent face, everyone was almost convinced, and were inclined to sympathize with him till someone in the group curiously asked "If this is the first time you drank, how come you could have so much of it?" Subranil smiled and calmly replied, "Good question! Well, what I really meant was that after the last time I had drinks, this was the first time!"

His colleagues burst out laughing. It took some time for them to understand what he was saying, and then the guys gave him a good beating screaming, "We'll make sure that 'this first time' will be your last time!"

The Brain

This is a very interesting incident. It highlights the fact that the brain is not a machine. It needs rest and if deprived of it, it can malfunction!

Dilip was a hardworking guy. But because of the project release he had been putting much more effort at work. The team had now been working for two days with bare minimum sleep.

Their bodies and brains were getting exhausted and the team members had started showing the symptoms of the deprivation. It was half past two in the night. The project had to be released to the client the next morning.

Dilip was reviewing the design document for one last time. Everything was going well until this happened. He got stuck at one of the simple statements in the document.

This is what he read,

'This led the led to turn led.'

He was half asleep and his brain had already stopped working. He thought he had started hallucinating as he was reading the same word 'led' again and again and he thought if he spent one more minute there, he would go mad.

After a good night's sleep, the next morning when he was back in office, he opened the document, went to the same sentence he had got stuck at.

The statement now read,

'This led the led to turn red.'

And now it made a whole lot of sense to him. Because of exhaustion the previous day, he was reading 'red' as 'led'!

(The second 'led' in the sentence is an abbreviation of 'Light Emitting Diode')

The Fall

R am was good at sports and made it a point to take out some time for it no matter how heavy the work load was. There was a playing ground just in front of the main gate of his office premises.

On a weekend his team had come to play cricket there. Most of the guys had arrived on time and had started playing. Ram had bought a new bike that day and was coming to the field directly from the showroom.

To show off his new bike, he started waving his hands and calling his friends from the gate. While doing this, he forgot to take the turn ahead and hit the footpath barricade. His brand new bike toppled over along with him right in front of his mates.

Everybody tried their best to suppress their giggles as they watched him park his bike. He then silently went and stood at a fielding position. It was definitely not the grand entry he had planned to make!

The Recruitment

Harish had a progressive journey in his organization. Within a few years of starting his career, he had moved on to managing a team of fifty people.

As an added responsibility, he had also joined the panel of experts who used to travel to colleges for various campus recruitments. He underwent a two day basic training session on how to take interviews, and on what to look for in a candidate.

However, any interviewer, being a unique individual, has his own ways to go about it. Some would mainly look for technical skills in the candidates while some would pay more attention to the personality and the analytical skills of the candidate.

Harish also had his ways of assessing the candidates. Apart from the technical and theoretical skill check, he would never forget to ask a common question to every candidate he interviewed. The question was: "What are your strengths and weaknesses?" Although the answers varied, on a wider level, the replies had a lot of commonalities. Mostly the candidates would boast of their technical strengths, their communication skills, leadership qualities and so on.

During a particular visit to a college, Harish had already interviewed more than ten engineers, but was not happy with any of them. The next candidate was good at technical knowledge but Harish felt that he lacked agility. He then asked him the same old question "What are your strengths and weaknesses?" And the reply (some part of it) included: "I do not have any weaknesses, Sir, except that physically I am a bit weak."

Harish couldn't control his laughter and impressed with this 'creative and confident' response, the candidate was selected!

The Lock

Everybody in our office was worried. The reason was that our well loved colleague, Armaan, had not come to office. Not coming to office is not a big deal. But this guy was different. In the past four years that he had been working for the company, he had never ever taken any unplanned and uninformed leave, and had come to office perfectly on time every single day even if he had to leave late the previous night. Whenever unwell, he would call the manager early in the morning to inform him.

Unfortunately for us, his faulty cellphone (which was now unreachable) was the only way of contacting him.

Till the afternoon, nobody was taking it seriously but as the day passed and neither Armaan came to office nor did he call nor were we able to reach him on his phone, the team got a little concerned.

We (including our manager) decided to go to his house. He hailed from Haryana, and was staying in a rented house. When we reached his place, we found that the main door of his house was locked.

Exasperated, our manager cried out aloud, "Where the hell are you, Armaan?" And to our shock and surprise, a voice came from nowhere – "In front of you. Just that I am on the other side of the door!"

Armaan had been locked inside the house along with his dead phone. His roomie hadn't realized he was still inside before leaving, and Armaan hadn't heard his roommate locking the door behind him while leaving!

The Bank Balance

Nowadays every thing is e-enabled. Be it banking transactions, money transfers, bill payments or online customer support, the internet has revolutionized everything. Well, but we must remember that every coin has two sides to it.

Girish was working in his cubicle when he got a call from his landlord who had not received the rent for that month. Girish assured the landlord that he'd pay him by the end of the day. Since a cheque would have taken more than two days to clear, he decided to transfer the money online to his landlord's account. He logged in to his account on the bank's website and the moment he was through with the transfer, he got another call. This time it was his manager was calling him for an urgent discussion.

He forgot to lock his PC. His cabin mate, seeing his Citibank account opened, transferred all the money to his account. When Girish returned to his desk, he was shell shocked to see the balance in his account – a hundred rupees. He was almost crying and started complaining about a pain in his heart. Although he could have found out to which account the money had been transferred, the mind doesn't usually work in such situations!

Fearing that he might get a heart attack, his colleague pacified him and said, "Don't worry! Your money is safe… with me! I'll return it to you but only on one condition – you have to give us a party worth 1% of your savings."

The bill after the party was five thousand bucks. He had five lakhs in his account!

The Pronunciation

Shetty's boss sometimes used to pronounce 'es' as 'esh'. The boss was aware of this fact and with a little effort, could pronounce the words properly. However, during times of joy and more so during times of stress, pronunciation was the last thing he thought about.

The boss was under fire from his managers and the client for a huge deviation in the project schedules and deliverables.

He had just come out of one such firing session, when a new joinee knocked on his cabin door.

The conversation between them:

Boss: "Come in!"

Fresher: "Hello Sir"

Boss: "Hello!"

Boss: "Please have a shit (seat is what he meant!)

Fresher: "Umm... I didn't get you."

Boss: "I said 'Please shit here.'

Fresher: "Umm... Aa... Sir?" The fresher was almost crying in nervousness.

Boss: "Okay don't bother. Come, I'll introduce you to the team.

During the introductory session, the fresher was finally able to make out what the issue was.

And at the end of it, the fresher said, "It was a pleasure meeting you."

Boss: "Shame here!"

The Pretender

Sachin and Subbu were roommates and best friends too. Subbu had always been a mischievous kid from his childhood days and that didn't change even when he grew up.

Sachin was looking for a job change and had floated his resume in various job portals. He had been getting calls from various consultants and was scheduling his interviews accordingly.

Already knowing Sachin's field of interest and his likes/dislikes, Subbu couldn't resist playing a prank. Pretending to be a consultant, he called up Sachin and told him that his resume had been short listed for a job vacancy and he would be having his telephonic interview after two days. The consultant (Subbu) also mentioned that if he cleared this interview round, he would have to fly to the US within a week.

Sachin was very excited about it and was preparing hard for this interview. After two days he was anxiously waiting for the telephonic interview.

His phone finally rang and the interview went something like this:

Consultant: "Hello Sachin?"

Sachin: "Hello, yes."

Consultant: "Hey Sachin, you have been selected without the interview. We know you prepared really hard!"

Sachin: "@!$%%^^"

The best part was that Subbu never disclosed that he was behind it to Sachin. Sachin was so annoyed that he didn't go for any interview for the next two months.

The Pink Slip

Anil was very excited as this was going to be his first onsite trip. He had got his US visa stamped and was flying to New York for a year long project assignment at the client's location. A critical resource, he was welcomed by the client's complete team.

It took him just few days to settle in. It was a new place, and a new environment but he was able to adjust well. After being allotted a desktop, he collected some stationery from the common resource location. Some of the few things he picked were notepads, scribbling pads, 'stick it' pads, pens, pencils and the like.

Being very organized at work, he used to plan his activities in advance and always made a 'to do' list for his daily activities.

One day his PC was not working. He tried to contact the support person but could not reach him. He was advised by a colleague (from the client's side) to just leave a 'stick it' pad at the concerned person's desk with the message and he would do the needful.

Anil did that immediately. The issue got resolved but when he met this support guy, the response was very cold. Anil liked the idea of using stick pads; he would go and drop a note at the concerned person's desk. Suddenly the response from many of his teammates started deteriorating.

Even after an excellent performance, and good behavior, he was unable to take this kind of behaviour from the others. And the worst part that was bugging him was that he was not able to find the root cause of the issue.

One fine day, he was reading a news article on layoffs which read:

'100 employees given pink slips'.

His mind suddeny put two plus two together. The stick notes he had been leaving were pink in color!

Things were totally different after that. Anil had become the favourite.

The Wife

Varun was getting married. Luckily for him, the work load was less so he had been granted four weeks' leave.

After these never forgettable thirty days of leave, Varun was back in office. There was a visible glow on his face. His dressing sense had changed. He looked like a gentleman.

Being off from work for quite a while, he had to bring himself up to speed with the current state of the project and so he was very busy in meetings and discussions with his managers. He had been getting a call at his desk. While he was out busy in some meeting, his colleague, who used to share the same cubicle, picked the phone and asked who was on the line.

A woman's voice replied, "I am your wife". As a spontaneous reaction, this guy, a bachelor, asked, "Which wife?"

And before he could say anything else he heard a bang before the telephone line was disconnected.

As we can safely assume, Varun had a nice time at home that evening.

The Photo

Govind's eyesight was extremely weak. Since he was not comfortable wearing contact lenses, he used to wear spectacles. He had already been scheduled for a laser operation the coming month.

His team had gone on a weekend trip to Goa. The team was having loads of fun there amidst the breathtaking beaches and lush scenery.

At one of beaches, Govind lost his spectacles and since his eye sight was too weak, he was unable to recognize distant objects. After losing his pair of costly spectacles and not in a mood to enjoy the sea anymore, he started clicking photos for the team.

Suddenly, this guy was surrounded by a group shouting at him. What was the reason? It so happened that as the team was going farther into the sea, Govind, unable to spot them properly, he lost track of them and had started taking photos of strangers mistaking them to be his team mates.

The Clock

Arun used to wake up at 6 a.m. sharp (thanks to his accurate biological clock) in the morning and go jogging. He had been following this routine for the past six months. All his other roommates used to wake up late.

There was a product release in his project and he had been working all through the weekend and had not slept for the past twenty four hours. The product was successfully released on Monday and he came early from office that day.

Within minutes of reaching home, he was fast asleep in his bed. Suddenly he woke up at around 12:30 in the night, and as usual, thought it was 6 a.m. As it was winter time, the sun would rise only after, seven in the morning. Following his usual routine, he went out for jogging. He did notice however that it was a little darker than usual and that none of the other joggers whom he usually met, could be seen on the road.

Sensing something fishy, he cut short his jog and returned home. When he had a look at the clock, it said 1 o'clock.

He smiled sheepishly and quietly went back to sleep again.

The Red Indian

It's difficult to send group mails by typing everybody's email id separately. Lazy as Arvind was, he created distribution lists instead in which one just needs to add all the email ids in a list and give it an appropriate name.

Arvind had made two such distribution lists – one consisted of his batch mates, his personal friends and some 'close' colleagues. The other consisted of all his team mates, his Project Manager, project leaders, team manager and so on. The first list was used for personal mails and the second one for the official ones. Too lazy to think of different names, he kept very similar names for these lists.

He was forwarding a mail to his friends (the personal list).The contents of the mail were something like this:

'Hey guys, it's time to move on, lots of opportunities are waiting for you and me...'

With it he attached a list of job openings.

Erroneously, he sent that mail to the second mailing list which included all his team mates, managers etc. Within split seconds, he was called by his manager.

After coming out of his manager's cabin, all one could say was that he looked like a Red Indian!

The Reason

There have been many incidents involving people asking for release from a project for an onsite opportunity, or a different role, or putting in their resignation due to salary reasons or other professional reasons.

But this one was a weird one. Mahesh had been working on the same project for more than a year now. He had started losing motivation; his efficiency was getting affected and his productivity was declining. Being self-aware, he finally decided to go to his manager and ask for a release from the project.

Since he had been a key member of the team, the manager wanted to retain him and was ready to accept his terms which had been unknown till then to some extent. During the discussion, the manager praised him for all the work that he had done and expressed his interest in retaining him. He said "Mahesh, Do not worry... tell me frankly why you want to leave the project?"

Mahesh (mechanical engineer, already tired of zero gender diversity in his college years) replied, "Well then frankly speaking, there are no girls working on our project now, so I do not feel like working there any longer."

The manager, stunned with this response, replied, "Thanks for your frank response. Well frankly speaking, you are released from the project. Now 'I' don't feel like working with you any longer!"

My Message

I am glad that I could pen down these memorable incidents. It's my pleasure to share them with my friends, colleagues, and all the working engineers out there. Small but cherishable moments like these will neutralize your work day blues away.

As I share these light hearted incidents, I hope all you engineers, working under tremendous pressure, do not end up turning yourselves into machines. You are human beings – enjoy every moment of your life. Work hard but live, laugh and have fun along.

I keep hearing so much about IT and software engineers dealing with stress related problems every day. I just want you guys to take life a bit lightly, that's all.

My wish is to see happy and stress free engineers everywhere!

www.ingramcontent.com/pod-product-compliance
Lightning Source LLC
Chambersburg PA
CBHW071959170626
46813CB00005B/1934